To the childlike, both young and old,
both naughty and nice.

Treats & Retreats for Christmas

Mark R. Turner

Published by Mark R. Turner, 2024.

TREATS & RETREATS FOR CHRISTMAS

First edition. December 18, 2024.

ISBN: 979-8230673453

Written by Mark R. Turner.

Treats & Retreats for Christmas

Mark R. Turner

Published by Mark R. Turner, 2024.

This is a work of fiction. Similarities to real people, places, or events are entirely coincidental.

TREATS & RETREATS FOR CHRISTMAS

First edition. December 18, 2024.

ISBN: 979-8230673453

Written by Mark R. Turner.

Table of Contents

Preface 1
"The Lost Kids Spy Christmas" 3
About Group Reading this Story 31
A Kid Knocks in the Night 35
About a Live Reading of this Scene 43
Commentary on "A Kid Knocks in the Night" 45
Power of the Tiny Particle 49
Unconditional Love 57
The Wrappings of Christmas 63

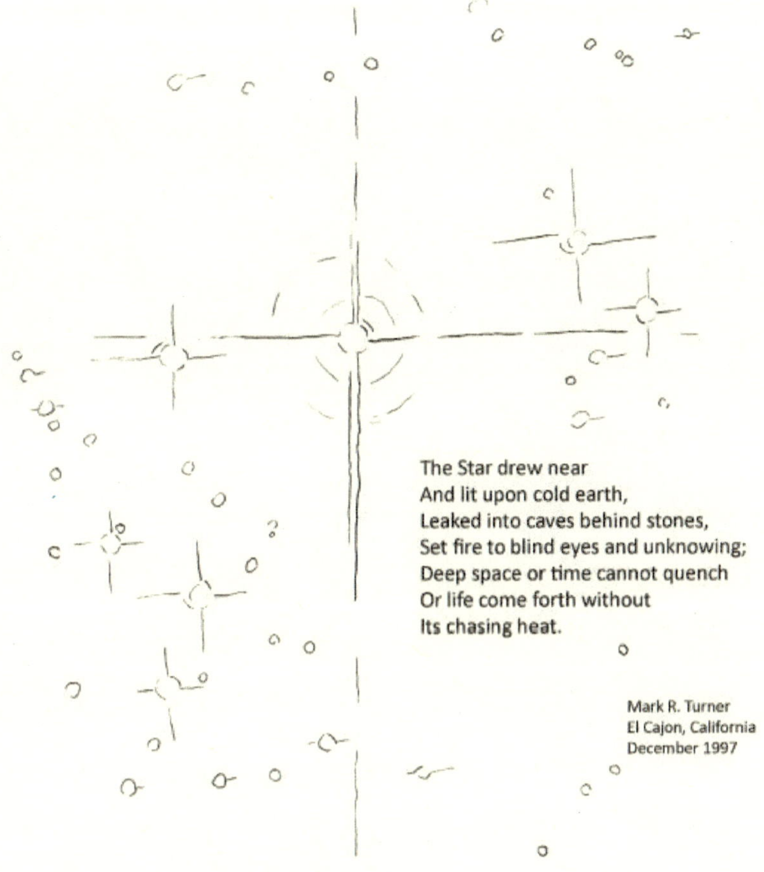

The Star drew near
And lit upon cold earth,
Leaked into caves behind stones,
Set fire to blind eyes and unknowing;
Deep space or time cannot quench
Or life come forth without
Its chasing heat.

Mark R. Turner
El Cajon, California
December 1997

Preface

This compilation spans decades of my Advent, Christmas and Epiphany experiences. From my earliest memories Christmas has held some of the most profound ideas and feelings of life; full of mystery, hope, and wonder about the past, present and future.

This season has always called for theatricality and these stories come from stage plays produced as explorations of the mysteries of the Nativity and how the modern world relates to it. The poetry indicates that the meanings of these celebrations push the limit of words; sometimes you just have to stop and feel that mysterious wonder. Indeed, I had to include some wordless imagery in drawings derived from more elaborate illustrations through the years.

But I am including some essays and commentary which have lots of words trying to discuss important aspects of what the seasonal celebrations address.

These offerings are an attempt to provide opportunities for pause and reflection. I hope you will take the time and even read aloud in the characters provided. There is music to be sung, poems for oration, funny twists of imagination, and dramatic crises to be confronted.

May you use these as platforms to launch out in discovery of your True Self, one more light filling the darkness.

Mark R. Turner

Advent 2024

The Lost Kids Spy Christmas

"Folks who live here in the air
Should not mix with folks down there.
They've got tales to turn your ear
All about this time of year.
Tales of angels in the night,
Baby king who brings us light.
From that stuff you must steer clear.
Listen to what we hold dear."

"The Lost Kids Spy Christmas"

by
Mark R. Turner

Two police officers cruise through the busy streets of the buzzing city. Late afternoon sun casts long shadows across old brick skyscrapers and flashes off glass walls. Cranston is new to the force. He keeps a sharp eye for infractions, unlawful motion, trouble. His partner, Berry, watches with a much more relaxed eye after fifteen years on the force. She glances at Cranston's grip on the wheel and his hard expression. "Cranston, you wanna live a little longer, you'll ease up."

"What? Tryin' to do a good job."

"I let you drive, didn't I?"

"Yeah. Thanks."

"We're not out here to save the world."

"Right. Gotta prioritize what we see. Gotcha."

Berry glances at him with a sympathetic grin. "There's no end to trouble. You gotta choose your battles."

Cranston slows the car. "Boss, hold on." He studies a young, teenage boy loitering on the corner. "You see what I see?"

"Yeah. He's one of 'em."

Cranston pulls the car over. Berry is already running way ahead of him. She yells, "Stop where you are, Joe!"

Joe sees the cops and disappears down the alley. Cranston yells, "Berry! This way!" Berry follows Cranston down the alley. They emerge at the other end winded, stop and search for the kid in the crowds of pedestrians and the rushing cars. Cranston kicks the building in fury. "We had 'im!"

Berry looks back down the alley. “Every time! They are some kind o’ smart, little sneaks!”

Cranston’s eyes darken with resentment. “We’ll flush those little punks out.”

“The academy teach you to talk like that?”

“Not this again,” Cranston complains as he follows Berry back to the car.

“I’m serious,” she says. “Is that all these kids are to you? Punks?”

“You wanna clean up this neighborhood, don’t you?”

“Not the point. Neighborhood is people.”

“That’s what I’m sayin’. Look at all these pu-—‘kids’ runnin’ around here. It’s no wonder all the pickpocketing and shoplifting.”

“You don’t just sweep all of ‘em into the trash.”

“You heard the Chief. The merchants are on his back.”

“They’re not all little thieves, Cranston. Don’t you think I been workin’ on this?”

“No offense, Berry, but I think there’s a reason the Chief put a younger guy right out of academy in your car.”

“Oh yeah? Well, I just happened to ask him for a youngster who could do the grunt work on this beat.”

“Right.”

“And you still follow my lead. I’ve been working on this case a long time and we’re looking for a particular group of kids.”

“You should’ve been a social worker, boss. We got a chance here to make a good mark for ourselves and the Chief and clean up the place.”

“You wanna just pick ‘em up and throw ‘em into the hall? Go ahead. Go on. Start pickin’ ‘em up, Cranston.”

“What’r ya—-“

“You can’t, can ya? The kids we’re after are like phantoms.”

“You seem to be familiar enough. You called him by name.

“Like I say, I been workin’ this case a long time.”

“You got kids of your own?”

“Jack and I are workin’ on that.” Berry pulls out some dollar bills, rolls them up and inserts them into a notch in the wall above a dumpster.

Cranston scowls at the wad in the notch. “What’s this?”

“It’s gettin’ to be kind of a tradition. Unorthodox, I guess.”

Cranston turns away melodramatically. "No. Don't tell me. Leaving money in the wall." He faces Berry with a sarcastic face. "Is this some kind of bait or something?"

"That was my original idea. Then I found a note in my pocket: 'Dear officer Berry, thanks for the donation. Signed, The Lost Kids.'"

Cranston grabs his face and turns away again with a snort. "Oh, you have got to be kidding me! You wanna know what I think?"

"No."

"I think you and Jack are gettin' so desperate for kids you're goin' soft on crime."

"You think there's no such thing as lost kids."

"Berry, it's gonna be okay. You'll be taking your pregnancy leave pretty soon and by the time you get back I'll have our little criminals behind bars."

"I'm not taking any pregnancy leave."

"I thought you and Jack were, like, 'working on it.'"

"Oh, yeah. We're getting certified to open a home for these criminals."

"What?" Cranston stares at her with a twisted face trying to comprehend.

"A good home." She gets into the driver's seat.

"Oh, don't get sappy on me, boss. Hey, I thought I was drivin'."

She pulls into traffic as he pulls his door closed.

On the rooftop of one of the older high-rise buildings is a collection of shacks and sheds pieced together from a hodgepodge of materials scavenged over years. Box gardens give ground to a veritable jungle of vegetables, flowers, and the sweet music of birds. Suddenly they take flight when a door bursts open and two young people run into the sunlight panting for breath. The young man is Joe, whom the officers nearly caught on the street. The girl is May, nearly a young woman, but wearing yesteryear's fashion.

Joe catches his breath and asks urgently, "Count 'em all?"

"Yep." May turns and watches the door. "Twenty-three in a row."

"What's keeping them?"

A kind of thunder fades up and out the door. Forty-six feet pounding and suddenly a crowd of kids from little to big bursts through the door. The kids horse around swinging bags full of things on their shoulders. The youngest congregate around May excitedly showing her the contents of their bags. She touches them each with encouraging hands.

Suddenly the largest apartment bursts open. "Wha———-at's the meaning of this!?" Yells a spry old man stepping out squinting.

The kids hush and scatter to hiding places from which to watch the old man. This is Ananiah, dressed in threadbare layers of clothing which were once bright and long ago considered fashionable. He stands like a mannequin shifting his eyes to and fro across his rooftop kingdom. Suddenly the kids all leap forward with glee toward Ananiah showing off the treasures in their bags.

Ananiah shouts mock epithets at them, "Aaaa! Wait! Wait, you monsters! One at a time, you scoundrels!" The kids back off giggling and trying to stand at attention. Ananiah strides back and forth before them. "You must learn to control your passions! Let us converse with civility." Ananiah straightens his spine and grasps his lapel. The kids all straighten their spines and stand in dignified poses. Ananiah strolls toward Joe. "And did you pass the time pleasantly down among the riffraff of the world?"

Joe raises his chin. "Indeed, most amicably."

"Good form, Joe. A model to the family."

The kids look at each other with puzzled faces repeating, "Amicably?"

Ananiah strolls on toward May. "And did you not find the surroundings tiresome and dreary this time of year?"

"On the contrary, sir," replies May. "We were quite taken with the gleaming opulence."

"Opulence!" he bellows. "My dear May, you're becoming quite the lady about town!"

The kids repeat the odd word, "Opulence?"

Joe reports, "They got everything decorated down there again, Ananiah."

One of the littlest shouts out, "Somebody said something to me down there and I don't get it!"

Ananiah grins down upon the child and stoops to her face. "And what did those evil beings say to you, my sweet?"

The girl's face twists with question, "They told me 'Merry Christmas.'"

Everyone gasps as one. May puts her hand over the child's mouth and stares at Ananiah. He shoots up to a straight stance in stiff agony as if being stabbed. "Aaaaaag! It isn't enough I make a home for you far above the city. No! You bring street talk right up to the roof top!" He peers down upon the child. "Now, being as this is your first venture down to the streets at this time of year, we'll let that pass. But it appears your education has been neglected." He turns sternly toward Joe. Joe steps forward sheepishly as Ananiah confronts him. "Have you been neglecting the new ones? Failing to verse them in the Why, Who and Wherefore of our daily lives?"

May steps up. "Ananiah, don't be hard on Joe. We've just been hearing these songs again and they make us sort of change."

Ananiah softens for May. "Yes, they do employ songs to get you!"

"Like the one," she begins to sing, "'Hark the herald angels sing, glory to the newborn—'"

Ananiah grabs his throat, "Aaaaaag! Stop! Stop! You've got it all wrong again. How many times must I tell you? Beware the Smujins and the Popagicies down on the street. The Smujins will say nice things to lure you away. The Popagicies will sing songs with the wrong words just to fill your heads with impossible dreams. Here. Here." He corrals the kids into a choir formation. "Get together now." He stands before them like a choirmaster at the local cathedral. "You know the words I taught you, words of truth about the real things which really matter." He raises his arms, and the kids take a deep breath. He throws his arms into the downbeat, and they launch into their version of the familiar Christmas carol.

"Folks who live here in the air
Should not mix with folks down there.
They've got tales to turn your ear
All about this time of year.
Tales of angels in the night,
Baby king who brings us light.
From that stuff you must steer clear.
Listen to what we hold dear."

Ananiah steps to one side as the kids pick up their bags. "Now, show your old Ananiah what you found for him today!"

The kids sing the next verse as they parade before Ananiah opening their bags and piling the contents in front of him.

"Pocket books with lots of cash,
Watches, wallets and hubcaps,
Pots and pans and ebook readers,
Baskets snatched from picnic eaters,
Shirts and sweaters, hats and coats,
Jewelry and mobile phones,
Laptops, cameras, credit cards,
Ear buds, smart pads, and guitars."

The kids whoop and cheer as Ananiah laughs and congratulates them. But May is more reserved, puzzling over things.

"Oh, yes, my loves!" effuses Ananiah. "You've all done your part to make our home a little brighter."

"But Ananiah," interrupts May. "Every year we've heard that song down there and it sounds a lot different."

"Now, my love—"

"There's that part about 'Peace on earth and mercy mild.'"

Ananiah searches his mind, "Oh, er, that's 'Fleece the earth New Jersey style.'"

She presses further. "But what does it mean 'God and sinners reconciled'?"

He thinks hard. "Uh, well, that's, uh, an old wrecking-recycling company. Yeah. Gottensiener Wrecking and Recycling."

"But what's the last line about? 'Christ is born in Bethlehem.'?"

"Ah, now give it a rest." Ananiah waves his "shoo" signal. "Everyone's got their chores! Everybody scram and get to work ... and no more daydreaming!"

Complaining, the kids scatter to various chores around the roof top, pulling out brooms, grabbing mops and rags. Some wash windows. Others sweep and dust. Still others work the garden. Ananiah works on the pile of goods which the kids brought him from the world below. He examines each item greedily as he carries it into his shack. When all the goods are in, he stays in, cataloging and pricing.

A woman wearing a bright bandana peeks around the door onto the rooftop. It is Meg and she lifts her eyebrows with a grin. "Yoohoo," she calls like some exotic bird.

The kids look up with delight, "The Swappers are here!" They drop what they are doing and run to greet three colorful, though worn, characters.

Meg laughs, "Ah, my pretty brats!"

Tess pinches cheeks and chins. "Sneaky-weekies."

Bunker hugs as many as he can. "Ah, you're good-for-nothin' lovies."

Meg is the boss of the Swappers. She wears the red coat on top of the green sweater on top of the yellow sweatshirt on top of the turquoise parka. She also sports an array of skirts of various prints and patterns with multi-colored shoes to match everything.

Tess is a veritable flower arrangement with straw daisies in her hat, silk irises woven into her sweater, plastic roses twisted together for a belt and a wild, floral print dress. She likes to make note of her floral shoelaces.

Bunker is more conservative and, seeing himself as a gentleman, wears three suits, the most appropriate one for the current occasion being the one on top, decorated with various shiny objects to draw attention to a prosperity which he calculates will engender respect.

Meg turns all around taking in the kids' faces. "So, we brung ya all somethin' fer the season." The Swappers open big bags which they have toted in. Out of the bags they pull a variety of toys and trinkets, giving each child a special gift. Turning to May as the last recipient, Meg looks into her eyes. "And because you all look up to May as the elder sis, we saved this 'til last."

Bunker pulls out a beautiful box tied with a ribbon and delivers it to May. She receives it with awe and pulls at the ribbon. Slowly the box opens. The kids gasp as she carefully lifts a perfect baby doll with real hair, smooth skin, and big eyes.

Ananiah storms out banging his door. "What's this?! Holding out on me again, Swappers?" He grabs the doll from May.

Meg counters the attack. "Aaa, pipe down!"

"It's the season!" yells Tess.

"I'll pipe you down!" retorts Ananiah. "What's the big idea giving away perfectly good merchandise?"

Bunker steps in. "Yeah, ya don't even know how to treat your own employees."

"Ha! Slaves!" corrects Meg. "Ya don't give holidays to slaves!"

May runs away into a shack crying.

"There!" rages Ananiah. "See what you've done to our peaceful home?" He thrusts the doll back into its box. "Raise the kids' dreams of opulence and dash 'em to the ground." He turns on the kids. "Everybody back to work!"

The kids scatter as fast as they can. Some of them sniff and a sob or two is also heard.

Ananiah grabs all three Swappers and pulls them to the side overlooking the city. "Have you goof balls completely drained that swamp you call a brain? What, in the name of Holt Dayton Hogsworthy are you tryin' to do? Kill our baby?"

Bunker perks up and looks around. "Baby?"

Meg bops his head. "The stash, nitwit."

Tess' eyes get a faraway look as she smiles greedily. "Our money baby."

"My baby!" Ananiah asserts. "Out of which I give you a cut providing I still like ya by then! And I'm not too optimistic of that right now, you fillin' all those little heads with ideas like they gotta get a present."

"Oh, 'Niah, sweets," Meg lays on the charm. "No harm meant. We figure they'll work harder if we give 'em a little tid bit."

Tess adds, "Especially when it's ... you know ..."

Bunker looks at them with bright eyes. "Christmas."

The all shush him angrily.

Ananiah leans into them. "Yes, and pretty soon you'll have 'em refusing to work unless you give 'em something for it? Where will it end? Ladies and gent, have you lost your vision? I remember when you used to look forward to taking your places among the rich and famous."

The Swappers' eyes grow wide as they gaze upon the city below.

Ananiah observes the trance he is placing upon them. "That's why we started feeding ... the baby."

The three Swappers build a musical chord one pitch at a time, "The baby ... The baby ... The baby"

They begin to waltz as they sing the tune of "We Three Kings".

"We three swells may stoop and may scratch
Don't look like we're much of a catch
What you see
Ain't royalty
But wait 'till our nest egg ha————tches.

"Feed the baby lots of cash

Make deposits in the stash
Grow that baby
And then maybe
We'll get rich and famous fast."

They laugh, cackle and dance around like chickens in the barn yard. Another chorus is irresistible.

"O————————h
Feed the baby lots of cash
Make deposits in the stash
Grow that baby
And then maybe
We'll get rich and famous fast."

Their laugh nearly chokes them.

"Alright, alright," Ananiah intervenes. "You can quit patting yourselves on the back now. You haven't moved any of this merchandise yet."

"Oh, we'll get a good price for that stuff," assures Meg. "You better start thinkin' how you're gonna make it up to May. She's one of your prime movers, you know."

"Treat her right and she'll do a lot to keep this merchandise flowin' in," adds Tess.

"Look, you three hawk it and I'll run the collection agency," reminds Ananiah turning to leave. "Now, feed the crew their supper." He disappears back into his shack.

Tess bangs on a pan. "Come and get it, Munshkins! Come and get it!"

The kids head over to Meg and Bunker who pull a cart out of a shed bearing stacks of bowls and spoons. A large pot is steaming with some kind of stew.

"Line up!" calls Bunker. "Line up for supper!" He starts dishing up the stew to the line of kids who hungrily take their bowls and spoons, sit down nearby, and gobble it down hoping for seconds. But soon they begin to quiz the Swappers.

Freckled Joni calls out, "Swappers, we heard this song down there."

Black Eye Will chimes in, "Yeah, we want you to teach it to us."

"Naaaa," objects Meg. "We don't know no songs."

"Sure!" counters Joe. "It goes something like ..." He searches for a pitch and May starts the song.

"It came upon the midnight clear—"

Meg jumps up. "Aaaaa Shad up!" The Swappers look back at Ananiah's shack nervously. Meg whispers, "Okay, okay. Keep it down!"

"We know the idiot song," Tess confides quietly.

Bunker gets the kids closer together. "Just, like real soft. Real soft and we'll give you a hand with it. Scoot over close." They pull everyone into a huddle. "So, it goes like this ..." The Swappers clear their throats and find the pitch.

"It came upon the midnight clear,

That glorious song of old."

Ananiah steps out. "What's this?"

The Swappers lean apart nervously. Bunker tries to fake it, "U—m, er—The Angels are the best ball club ..."

Tess takes over. "Yeah—The players drive cars of gold!" She turns to Meg who thinks fast and picks up the tune.

"If you'll be smart just like those guys,—" She looks to Bunker hopefully

And he starts without thinking, "You'll all ..."

Tess jumps in "... live like ..." then they all get the ending, "... kings and queens."

Ananiah keeps his eye on them as he slinks back into the shack. The Swappers and kids lean in as the song finishes stealthily.

"The world in solemn stillness lay

To hear the angels sing."

The Swappers drop to the floor with relief. May observes the Swappers skeptically. "That one didn't sound quite right either."

Joe agrees. "Yeah. The Angels don't sing. They play ball."

Tess takes up the challenge. "Well, originally they started out as a ..." But she falters.

Bunker saves her, "Men's chorus."

"Off season like," Tess adds unconvincingly.

"Shad up!" cuts in Meg. "Time for bed!" They start getting the kids to their feet. "Come on."

The kids are so weary that they can hardly get up to make their way to bed.

Joe yawns. "Bunker, will we really live like kings and queens?"

"Oh, yeah," Bunker assures him. "Just hang on. We'll all be rich."

Toothless Jenny rubs her eyes, "What'th a tholemn thtillneth?"

Little Ernie insists, "Yeah. I don't get about the ball club."

Lori pulls on Tess's dress. "Do they really drive gold cars?"

"Shad up! Shad up!" warns Meg. "You want the ol' man to turn us all into guacamole? Lay down there."

The kids fall into bed.

"Yeah, you can dream up all your answers, lovies," Tess reassures them.

"Nighty-night, tiddlywinks," calls Bunker as he closes the door of the shack and joins the other Swappers descending the stairs from the rooftop.

Joe lays still in the dark looking up through the cracked window at the stars. "Hey, May, how come you ain't satisfied with the songs like they sung 'em?"

May is sitting up against the wall. "Don't sound as good as the ones down on the street."

"Maybe you're getting too old for this racket."

"Something is going on that we don't know about."

"Of course. Lots of things."

"No, I mean why would the Swappers bring us presents?"

"Sorry about your doll."

"Yeah. That's the closest I ever came to anything like that."

"Me too."

"Why are the stores all decorated, and people singing special songs on the streets? Something is going to happen that Ananiah doesn't want us to know about."

Joe lets out a big yawn. "Night, May. Go to sleep." He turns over and is out.

May folds her arms as she sits thinking. Far away she can hear occasional, faint car horns in night traffic. Why, on winter nights, are they running around so late down there?

In the middle of the night a kindly looking woman quietly watches May from across the room. May looks up and slowly turns toward the woman. "Who's there?"

"I am honored to meet the great May of the Rooftop," says the woman. Her voice is almost like hearing music.

May is a little nervous and she confronts the woman. "Who are you? How did you get up here?"

"Well," says the woman softly. "I don't come from down on the streets."

May eyes her thoughtfully. "I've never seen you around here."

"But you notice me now."

May catches her breath. "You're Ananiah's secret."

This humors the woman. "He has lots of secrets and we will deal with those. As for me, you may call me Gabriella. I have a very important message to give you."

"You want to tell me what's going on? That's different around here."

Gabriella comes closer to May's bed. "May I sit with you?"

May gives her room on the bed.

Gabriella sits and tells May, "I saw you lose that beautiful doll."

"I been looking at those dolls in the stores."

"There is another which no one wants."

"Think of that. And me up here with nothing."

"This one is not really a doll. It's a real baby."

"Wait a minute. You aren't selling babies. 'Cause Ananiah doesn't take anyone under five years old."

"This is not for Ananiah. It is you who are chosen to take care of this unwanted baby."

May studies Gabriella skeptically. "Right under Ananiah's nose I'm gonna have a baby."

"Ananiah has eyes to see but he does not see; ears to hear but he does not hear."

"So, he's not gonna notice? Well, yeah, that wouldn't surprise me. But look, do you know how old I am?"

"I've seen how you look after the others. And I know your heart."

"Can Joe and the others help?"

"They are the other reasons you are chosen. It will take all of you."

"And we're the only bunch you want to give this baby to?"

"It's you or nobody."

May gets up and paces, thinking it over. The woman watches hopefully until, finally May turns to Gabriella. "I guess we better do what we can."

"I'm glad you accept, May. Come and lie down. You'd better get some sleep. This is going to be a handful."

"Now I can't sleep."

Gabriella puts her hand on May's cheek. "How about if I sing that midnight song the way it really goes? I can assure you it has nothing to do with baseball."

May relaxes on her pillow. "You know it?"

"Know it? I lived it." She begins to sing softly.

"It came upon the midnight clear,
That glorious song of old,
From angels bending near the earth
To touch their harps of gold:
Peace on the earth, goodwill to men,
From heaven's all gracious King.
The world in solemn stillness lay
To hear the angels sing."

May stretches out under the covers and closes her eyes. "I am so tired. But I want to hear the rest of the song." She feels as if she is floating. Gabriella's voice is the wind. She seems to hear the rest of the kids singing too.

"And you, beneath life's crushing load,
Whose forms are bending low,
Who toil along the climbing way
With painful steps and slow,
Look now! For glad and golden hours
Come swiftly on the wing;
O rest beside the weary road,
And hear the angels sing."

Gabriella rises from May and moves noiselessly among the beds touching the children's heads as she leaves the dormitory shack.

In May's dreams Ananiah has put up curtains and, beside her bed, a lamp with a fancy lamp shade all to make a proper home for the doll which the Swappers have given her. And here the doll is close to her, wiggling in his sleep. Surprising that a doll can kick like that ... two little feet nudging one at a time in a steady rhythm ... May opens her eyes wondering who is in her bed. There beside her a bundle of baby blankets wiggles. May stares at the bundle. She gasps. "This can't be a doll." She slowly, carefully reaches for the blanket and folds it back. There a small, round face looks up at her with big, clear eyes. "Look at you. Better than a dream." May sits up and eases the baby into her arms. The two of them sit looking contentedly at one another.

One by one the other kids wake up and notice the bundle in May's arms. They gather around with "oo's" and "ah's", entertained by the presence of such a little one.

Joe is the last to wake up. "Hey, what's up? What's the attraction?" He opens the crowd around May's bed and sees the baby. "What!? What's a baby doin' -—Where'd you come up with a stupid baby, May?"

"He's not stupid," she retorts.

"Yeah, well this ain't no place for babies. Ananiah's gonna blast us."

"Maybe we shouldn't tell him."

"Right. Keep a baby secret. You're out of your mind."

Gabriella speaks from behind the group. "Ananiah won't see this baby."

The kids turn around in surprise and Joe jumps toward Gabriella ready to fight. "Hey, you! How'd you get in?"

"Wait, Joe," May intervenes. "This is Gabriella."

He keeps his eyes on the intruder. "I don't know any Gabby-whatsit. How do we know she ain't after that baby?"

Gabriella interrogates Joe. "You ready to fight for that baby?"

Joe lunges at Gabriella with a threatening face and fists up.

Gabriella does not move. "Yes. I think you'll do. You are May and the baby's new bodyguard."

The kids burst into cheers and crowd around Joe. Gabriella hands Joe a package of diapers. "You'll be needing these."

Joe takes the package, looks at May and the baby, then turns back to find Gabriella gone. "Hey, where'd the lady go? And don't crowd the kid. A little air, guys. A little air."

Ananiah rushes in with the day's business on his mind. "Alright, alright, everybody up and at 'em! The Swappers have your oatmeal piping hot. Everybody out for breakfast! Let's go!"

The kids continue to huddle around May and the baby as if they never heard Ananiah.

He scowls at them. "I said—-!"

They all turn to him trying to block his view of the baby. In unison they politely greet him, "Good morning, Ananiah."

"Playing house at the break of dawn? Everybody but May get out for breakfast." He chases them all out but turns to find Joe still standing by May. "You too, Joe. Beat it."

Joe searches for a response. "Oh, I'm supposed to guard ... um ... them."

"Cute, Joe. Play the daddy later. It's a bright day; lots to do; pockets to pick." He chases Joe out with a raised fist then turns to May. He lingers nervously searching for the right words. "So. May, my pride and joy. I see you've made up a bundle to replace the doll that escaped your grasp." He inserts a chuckle. "Well, never fear. I've reconsidered." He pulls the doll out of a bag and presents it to her. "Let it not be said your old Ananiah never rewards his kids."

May accepts the doll with an appreciative smile. "Thank you. That's very thoughtful, Ananiah. You're the first person to give anything to the baby." She shows the doll to the baby. "He loves it. Don't you, little sweetheart? Yes, you do."

Ananiah eyes the bundle in her arms. "Uh ... er ... the baby." He comes close and looks into the bundle. "Right. Uh ... the baby. Well, I guess you got a doll of each kind now: real and invisible. Leave 'em here and get out to breakfast."

May says, "I'll be right out after I change him."

He eyes the bundle and observes May smiling down into it, then leaves shaking his head.

The kids keep an eye on the dormitory shack as the Swappers fill their bowls with oatmeal. They whisper to each other about the baby and expect Ananiah to blow up any second. But nothing happens and May strolls out for breakfast carrying the baby bundled in the blankets.

Meg sides up to one of the little kids who is noisily gobbling his oatmeal. "Say, Gregory, what's all this whispering about a baby?"

Gregory looks up out of the side of his eye suspiciously. Meg waits a little nervously and tries to keep a big smile.

"Well," says Gregory. "Promise you won't tell?"

She broadens her smile. "I'm zip lipped."

"Okay. Well, see, May got a real baby from someplace last night."

Meg is stunned but it does not affect her smiling face. "Did she, now? Well, ain't that a blessing." She pats Gregory on the head and unobtrusively makes her way to Tess and Bunker. She whispers, "Hey, Tess. Tess. Pssst. Over here. Bunker, Get over here."

"Yeah, Meg," Tess says distractedly. "I gotta wash up, you know."

Bunker trots over. "Yeah, boss. What's up?"

"Get this," confides Meg, eyeing Ananiah's shack. "'Niah's been holding something out on us. They got a baby."

"Yeah," says Bunker. "The money baby."

"No. Not that one," says Meg irritated. "A real one. Look at May holding that bundle over there."

Tess's eyes grow wide, and she sucks in a slow gasp. "Do you realize what you can get for one of them on the baby market these days?"

"You're readin' my mind, sister. If we could make that sale on our own, we could skip the old man's cut."

"Good," says Tess. "I got some contacts who can set us up with some rich couples in the market for babies."

Bunker is hesitant. "But what if we look at the little punkin and he's cute and lovable and sweet and dear and we wanna keep him? What then?"

Meg and Tess glare at him in silence. "Don't look at it," they explode over him.

"We just keep it wrapped up and don't pay it no mind. See?" instructs Meg. "'Cause babies is dangerous."

"Dangerous and devious," adds Tess.

"Yes, they'll get under your skin," agrees Bunker. "They'll do that."

Meg lifts her finger like a professor. "Let's review what we've learned about this sort of thing."

The Swappers clear their throats and find a pitch.

"Verse 1, to the tune of 'Away In A Manger,'" directs Meg. They all sing:

"Away with the babies. Now don't take a chance.
The darlin's will hypnotize you with a glance.
Don't ever look down in their cute little face.
They'll capture you and take charge of the whole place."

They adjust their stances and renew their concentration. "Verse two," directs Meg. They all pick up the melody again.

"If your baby's trying to look in your eye,
It's time to find shoppers awaiting to buy.
You get a good price for those bundles of love
And no dirty diapers when push comes to shove."

They burst into private cackles trying to keep inconspicuous.

Ananiah appears. "Alright, alright, stop that cackling over there and wash up. You kids, it's time for the highlight of the day. Off to the streets. Come on. Come on."

The kids stack their bowls and spoons and parade past May to say good-bye to the baby. Ananiah fumes at them. "And you can stop the phony baby game! May, I thought I told you to leave the dolls on your bed."

"I left the doll there," she says.

He is getting irritated. "My love, you can't mess with that one on the job."

"But he hasn't eaten yet and as soon as I get a bottle and formula, he's going to have breakfast."

"It's a cute little game, little mommy, but—"

Joe rushes May and the baby out the door. "It'll be alright, Ananiah. I'll give her a hand. Bye!" Joe and May are the last ones down the stairs.

Ananiah growls and turns on the Swappers. "Well, get this breakfast stuff cleared away!" He stomps into his shack grumbling, "Those kids are gonna drive me insane before I can get ..."

The Swappers look at each other with conspiratorial grins. Meg rattles off the plan, "Tess, you get your wrap and go on after those contacts of yours. Bunker and I will stay back and wash up."

They all stop and look with excitement at each other.

"The baby," says Tess.

"The baby," says Meg.

Bunker looks out dreamily, "Ain't they just darlin'?"

Tess and Meg bop him on the head. "Sshhh! Don't think about that!"

"Ow! You don't have to whop me on the head!"

On the street Joe and May have obtained a baby bottle and formula. "I figured that church would have something," says Joe.

May watches the baby gulp at the bottle. "He sure likes the stuff."

"I don't know, May," says Joe looking around nervously. "We shouldn't be just standing around with a baby down here." What he is feeling is the eyes of officers Berry and Cranston.

"Oh no," May says under her breath. She averts her eyes casually. "Take a look down at the corner."

Joe snatches a look. "Officer Berry," he says mildly. "And that new cop," he adds with disgust.

Down at the corner Cranston feels the thrill of a chase coming up. "Ho, ho, ho. Looks like Santy Claus is gonna be good to us today. Eh, Berry?"

"Hmmm," analyzes Berry. "Joe and May. The oldest of them. Let them lead us to the others."

"Looks like the girl's already got a bunch of stolen goods."

Berry is cautious. "Don't get too eager, Cranston. Let them lead us to the others."

"Aaaa. Stick in the mud." Cranston is antsy.

"Cranston, don't you move 'till I make the call," warns Berry.

Cranston takes a few steps toward Joe and May. "Get while the gettin's good."

Joe notes the developments. "Start walking."

May lets out a worried sound.

Berry raises her voice, "Cranston, I am warning you. Get back here."

Cranston turns to Berry. "And I'm warning you. If this comes up in an inquiry, I will make sure you are deep fried for paying delinquents money and refusing to apprehend them." He turns and moves toward Joe and May at a quick pace.

Joe quickens his pace. "Pick it up, May. They're on to us."

May looks for crowd cover, but pedestrians are not very plentiful yet.

Berry keeps up. "Insubordination, Cranston. You want that on your record?"

"I'll out-weigh that by capturing some of these brats." He starts a fast trot.

"Run, May," says Joe.

They take off running.

Cranston yells, "Get those brats!"

Berry calls to the kids, "Wait, Joe! May!"

The kids duck around the corner, dodging pedestrians and vehicles. They have gained a few seconds on the officers. Then Joe spots Tess. "Look! Tess's over there!"

Tess just happens to be on the kids' route and particularly helpful. "What is it, kids!?"

"Tess! You gotta help us! The cops!"

Cranston rounds the corner and Tess spies him pausing to get his bearings. "Aa. The new punk, huh? The lady cop will be around soon. I'll send 'em south. You duck in here. Give me the baby and meet me back home." She reaches for the bundle.

But May pulls back searching Tess' face. "Oh. But, he's my responsibility."

Tess plays hardball. "You wanna lose the baby altogether? Take the long route to throw the cops while I get the baby safe to home. Don't argue."

May kisses the baby and carefully lays the bundle into Tess' arms. "Be careful and I'll see you right away at—-"

"Beat it, kids," says Tess. "He spotted you!"

They run into the alley. Cranston takes off after them, but Tess waves him down. "No! They went this way!"

Cranston glances skeptically. "Right, lady. I'll be back for you! He disappears into the alley.

Berry runs up to Tess. "Excuse me, ma'am—"

"Morning, officer," says Tess in an attitude ready for a long conversation. "After someone?"

"My partner's chasing two kids," Berry says hurriedly.

"Oh, there's lots of little punks on these streets. Disgraceful."

"A boy about 10 or 11, a girl maybe about 12."

"How's a lady to raise a newborn?"

"Ma'am, I'm on the run. Which way did they go?"

"Aren't you hard. Yeah, I saw 'em. They went up that way." She points the opposite direction from Joe and May's route and Berry takes off that way.

"Okay, love ya. Bye-bye," sings Tess with a wave and a chuckle. "Idiot."

Joe and May walk lightly along a certain alley. "Hold it," whispers Joe. "Just hang back a second. Make sure no one's snooping around."

They try to blend into the dumpsters and junk piled along the side of the alley. Cranston stays low and creeps up behind a bale of cardboard. He grins congratulating himself that the kids do not see him.

Joe looks around and comes up with a plan. "Wait here. I'll get the window." He strolls casually across the alley to a stack of crates. He looks around again, then pushes the crates slightly away from the wall revealing a basement window. May scurries over, they push the window open and slip down into the dark. Cranston giggles quietly as he watches Joe's hand pull the crates back against the wall. "Aha!"

"What, 'aha'?" Berry says over Cranston's shoulder.

He jumps back startled and turns on Berry angrily. "Damn it, boss! Don't do that!"

"What's the 'aha'?" she repeats.

"Nothin'."

"What are you sneaking around here for?" Berry shoots a warning glare at Cranston.

Cranston straightens his clothes and assumes a dignified posture. "This is gonna be my bust and my promotion."

"You withholding information, officer?"

He has a subtle, cocky bounce to his stride. "You can come along, if you want, when I swoop down on the whole gang. Or you could wait and see my picture in the news."

Berry looks around in anger then turns and follows Cranston.

Back on the rooftop May is pacing and biting her nails. Joe watches with concern. "May, would you quit walking around and relax?"

She frets, "Tess should've been here before us with the baby. It's been over an hour. I should never have trusted her."

The soft thunder of the kids returning up the stairs diverts their attention. The kids burst through the door but not in their usual rowdy way. They are on a mission calling Joe and May.

"What are you guys doing up here now?" Joe demands.

Freckled Joni tries to catch her breath, "You guys, the Swappers got the baby!"

"We know that! Where are they?"

Little Ernie holds the sides of his head. "Oh, this is bad. This is really bad."

Black Eye Will takes over. "Listen. Me and Little Ernie was working by the park, and we saw Tess with the baby dialing a call."

Little Ernie butts in, "We snuck up to hear and she was phoning someone about buying the baby!"

May grabs the boy, "They're selling our baby?!"

Joe steps over to the door. "Where are the rats?"

Ernie pries loose from May, "They were talking about meeting in the back room of Brannigan's Shoe Shop right away."

Joe rallies the gang. "Okay, everybody, let's get 'em."

"Ah, my loves!" cries Ananiah stepping in from downstairs. The kids gasp and back away as he advances. "So early in the day? Taking a break from the toil of the streets? Run out of rich pickings, did we?"

May steps up to him. "Ananiah, something terrible has happened to the baby!"

Ananiah's face goes white. He rushes into his shack. A series of crashes and thuds follows. Then silence. Ananiah slumps out the door again a little faint. "My dears, would you please not do that to my poor heart. You'll be happy to know that the baby is fine."

"No," shouts May. "Not your stupid treasure! Our real baby that came in the night. You've got to help us get it back!"

Ananiah grimaces and almost weeps. "N——o! Not that game! Not this time of year when the biggest crowds are walking the streets and packing the stores with their pockets, bags and satchels full; the time when the picking is the sweetest, the harvest is the ripest and the bounty is plenteous."

Joe knows what will bring him to his senses. "It's the Swappers, Ananiah!"

Ananiah grabs Joe, "What's thi——s!?"

Joe presses in, "They're out selling something you don't know about."

Ananiah chokes. "No! Aaaag! Trying to get ahead of the old man, are they?"

May states her case. “Ananiah, you have your baby and now you know how we feel about ours. We’ve worked for you all this time. Can’t you help us save our baby from being sold?”

For the first time Ananiah feels comradeship with his little partners. “Hmmmmmmm,” he schemes. "I’m a reasonable man. I don’t take kindly to those what hold out on my partners in business. Where did you say we’d be meeting with them?”

“Back room at Brannigan’s Shoe Shop,” Joe rattles off.

“Hmmm,” continues the old man. “Old Brannigan’s got a business on the side, eh?” He reaches for his company. “Draw near, my pets, and hear my plan ...”

In a dingy little room smelling of shoe leather the Swappers arrange a small table and chairs for their meeting. “You think you guys can make it look good?” demands Meg.

“Better believe it,” assures Tess. “Our chance to make some real cash.”

Bunker holds the baby in the bundle all covered up. He’s been real curious to see what it looks like. “Maybe I better take a look at the baby and—-”

“Don’t look at the baby!” Meg and Tess jump at him.

Meg instructs them. “The little couple will be here any minute. Don’t mess up.”

Tess is anxious. “Any idea what they look like?”

“Who cares? I know what their money looks like.”

Bunker looks at them with concern. “Well, we want them to look like parents.”

“You don’t look like that until a few years after you bought your kid,” Tess informs him.

A knock rattles the door.

“There they are,” whispers Meg. “Okay, look dignified.”

Tess and Bunker strike poses.

Meg sneers. “Forget it! Just look like you own an orphanage. I’ll bring them in.” Meg opens the door. “Mrs. Doonhunkle?”

Mrs. Doonhunkle is dressed in a full length, beige gown and gloves. Her long, curly hair, hat and veil obscure her face giving her an air of mystery. She is curt with them. "Good afternoon." She gracefully glides into the room.

Bunker holds the baby closer. He doesn't think this one looks very motherly.

Meg speaks as formally as she can manage. "Please excuse our temporary office while we're remodeling thanks to your gracious tax dollars."

The lady returns, "And you'll have to excuse my husband, Emerson. He was unable to come, but he is very interested in babies."

"Ah, indeed," says Meg, bowing. "We shan't let a thing like that nix, er disrupt the job, er, proceedings. Let me introduce my associates: Madam Phi Beta Kappa and Sir Roundabout Wholesomeness. I'm sure you've heard of them in the world of baby lore."

"An excruciating honor to be sure," says the lady.

"Now, Mrs. Doonhunkle," Meg hurries on. "I am most certain that you are looking forward to having your first child, aren't you?"

"Oh, how did you guess?"

"Only a woman knows, right?" figures Meg. "I can see it all over you."

The lady giggles girlishly. "You can?"

Meg feels she has the upper hand now. "But, before I lay the baby in your motherly arms, there is the little matter of the ... er, fees."

"Oh, I never buy anything without seeing it first," explains Mrs. Doonhunkle.

Meg stops and thinks. "You wish to ..."

Tess finishes for her. "...look at it?"

"Just a peek," the lady returns with dignity. "You know, kick a tire, slam a door, see if it works."

Meg straightens up and cautiously gives instructions. "Sir Wholesomeness bring forth the baby. Mrs. Doonhunkle has volunteered to ..."

Tess finishes for her. "... look into the baby's face."

Bunker looks at the veiled lady resentfully and steps over to her. He bends down to show the baby. Meg and Tess cover their eyes with one hand and cover Bunker's eyes with their other hands. Mrs. Doonhunkle lifts the blanket from the baby's face and peers down at it. Suddenly she is outraged. "Ha! What's this? Some kind of joke?" She drops the blanket back.

The Swappers straighten up in surprise. "Madam doesn't like the color?" queries Meg.

"If my husband were here, he'd beat you up."

"Perhaps it's the size that doesn't please," suggests Meg hastily. "I have a fine selection of other kids to choose from."

Suddenly Mrs. Doonhunkle's voice becomes gruff, low and ... familiar. "Oh, you do, do you?!" Mrs. Doonhunkle pulls her hair off!

The Swappers watch in horror. "Aaaaaaaaaa!" Mrs. Doonhunkle is morphing into ... Ananiah!

"I've had enough of this," shouts Ananiah. "You good-for-nothing child racketeers! Gimme that thing!" He grabs the baby from Bunker. The kids charge into the room yelling. The Swappers run around the room in a panic and out the door screaming. The kids cheer and laugh until they think they will split.

When Ananiah can get the words out, he savors the moment. "Did you see their faces when I yanked off my hair?"

Everyone commences another bout of laughter. Finally, Ananiah catches his breath. "Here you go, May. Here's your little bundle." He lays the baby into May's arms.

May looks down into the blanket to find the baby enjoying all the commotion. "There's our baby. There you are. He's smiling!" She turns to Ananiah. "You have done a wonderful thing for us, Ananiah."

"Ha!" he responds. "It takes very little to make my kids happy." He falters and sits down to rest.

May comes close. "You okay, Ananiah?"

"It's a lot of work for that little bundle of blankets," he confides with a weak smile.

"You can't see the way we see, can you?" May sympathizes. "I guess you lost your Swappers."

"The old troublemakers!" he says. "They were actually going to sell me one of you!" They all laugh at the thought. Ananiah gets quiet. "Nope. Maybe it's time to retire."

May puts her hand on his old shoulder. "You need to rest. Let's get out of this dingy room. Joe, give him a hand. Let's all get back home for an early supper." Ananiah leans on Joe, and they all file out with customary stealth through the shadows to their rooftop home.

The kids make Ananiah comfortable as May and Joe put together some supper. After supper they kick their shoes off and lounge around their roof top oasis. Ananiah peruses all the young faces with a sense of melancholy. May sits by him feeding the baby another bottle. "You're thinking," she ventures.

"Ah," Ananiah rallies himself. "Just about old times."

"What did you do when you were a kid?" she probes.

"Oh, I was just remembering my mom's decorations this time of year," he muses.

The kids look at each other with surprise. "What did she put out?" May cautiously pursues.

"I remember when I was little, one of the only things I can remember about my ma was a nativity set. She'd put it out every Christmas."

Everyone is focused on Ananiah's nostalgia. He rises and begins placing the kids as he describes his old nativity set. "May, you and the baby would be right here." May sits there with the baby. "And, Joe, you come over by her and make the little Christmas family." He enjoys the scene. "Joe and May and the baby Jesus in a little shack place."

He shows some others where to pose. "Then we'd put the donkey and the cow. And over here, you and you be the shepherds come from the hillsides because they had heard about ... at any rate they brought you and you to be the sheep ... and you three, we'd set the three kings with their camels, you guys go be the camels right to the side about there." He stands back and inspects the little tableau the kids are presenting. "But tonight, the scene's not quite right, somehow."

Ananiah sits down and sings his own version of "Away In A Manger".

"I've worked all my life amassing wealth
By cheating, conniving, backstabbing and stealth
Yet, now, on the threshold of a gilded estate
The horrified feeling is I am too late."

He cannot quite put his finger on it, but something feels missing from the scene. Gabriella walks in and stands near Joe and May where the angel would be in the nativity scene. Ananiah recognizes her. "There you are. I haven't seen you since, oh, my, since I was just a little kid. You came and told me about the, um, that lady next door with the baby. What was it? A blanket they needed, right?"

Gabriella smiles at Ananiah. "It was a good Christmas when you brought them that blanket, Ananiah."

He thinks back. "Haven't seen you since you warned me to steer clear of the gang. They all died years ago. I suppose you come to take me, now."

She points to the baby held in May's arms.

He contemplates the kids. "Yes. I've put together the only kind of family I know: a gang of crooks and thieves."

She continues to point. "You have eyes to see. Use them."

Ananiah creeps closer to May and the bundle. He kneels, looks down into the blankets and catches his breath. "There ... there really is a ..."

Gabriella speaks softly. "Ananiah, now can you see the final thing missing from the nativity scene?"

He nods with a reluctant smile, then gets Joe to help him up on account of his creaky knees. "Now that we have the real baby, we'll give him the phony one. Wait here." He turns and goes into his shack. The kids look at each other listening to the clanks and thuds inside. He returns dragging a chest and drops it with a clunk beside May and the baby. "There. That's for the three kings' presents in the nativity scene."

Joe looks at Ananiah with a grin. "I guess you told us about Christmas, huh, Ananiah?"

"Kids, you know what I got for Christmas? I got my eyes opened. 'Cause you let Jesus in. I'm almost too late, but ..." He opens the chest to reveal a stash of money bags. He starts distributing the bags to each child. "Now, each of you knows how to take from people. It doesn't take nearly as much practice to get good at giving. So, off you go before it gets dark sssand—"

Before he gets it out the kids noisily take their bags of money and rush down into the streets. They know what to do with it. Ananiah stands with Gabriella rocking the baby and singing as he watches the kids pass out all the money to all the flabbergasted pedestrians below until not a dollar is left!

Having completed their mission, the kids gather at the secret entrance to return home. Suddenly police sirens fade in and glaring lights come rushing down the alley, screeching to a halt on both sides of the kids. Officers jump out. "I got you this time, ya little brats!" Cranston shouts triumphantly. "Come on, boys! Over here, news cameras!"

"Not so fast, Cranston!" It is officer Berry's voice. "Stay where you are officers. I've got full custody of these kids."

"That's impossible!" yells Cranston.

"Here's the papers fresh from downtown. You'll also find in there the reason I'm retiring from the force."

"Oh yeah?"

"Yeah. Jack and I, we got approved to open a home for these kids."

Joe yells out, "Nice goin', Officer Berry!"

The kids cheer and applaud.

But this does not stop Cranston. "Now, you just slow down. I think, if you will take a peek in this here hideout, you will find some serious evidence which will put this bunch in a tougher place than your little home."

"Go ahead, officers," calls Joe. "You won't find nothin' 'cept the ol' guy that took care of us."

Ananiah walks into the crowd carrying the baby. He places him in May's arms. May carries the baby over to Cranston. "This is the only treasure we have, Officer." She pushes the baby into Cranston's arms.

"Hold it!" Cranston protests. "Wait a minute. I never held a –" Something in the blanket arrests his attention. "Whoa, he's a jolly critter, isn't he." He instinctively rocks the baby. He cannot avert his eyes and his professional grimace melts into a smile.

May brightens at the sight of Cranston's transformation. "That's like the joy song we hear down here."

"Joy song?" Cranston looks up. "You mean 'Joy to the World'? That's a classic." He sees the kids' quizzical stares. "Yeah, you know." He sings the first line of the song, "Joy to the World the Lord is come ... Like that." The baby giggles and reaches for Cranston's chin, which makes the officer laugh, "He likes it!"

Little Ernie blurts out "Ananiah has other words for that song."

"No, no, now listen to the officer," Ananiah shouts hastily. "Please, keep singing, officer."

"Yeah," shouts Officer Berry. "Everybody sing! Cranston yell out the words!"

So, the alley echoes with the first time the lost kids have ever sung the real "Joy to the World" and Cranston feeds them the lyrics like he has found his real calling as a vaudeville song leader.

About Group Reading this Story

"The Lost Kids Spy Christmas" was originally produced as a stage play in the early 1990's and again as a reader's theater play in 2005. You can have fun reading it as a group by dividing up all the characters, one to a part, or between as few as six readers in the following distribution: 1.) Cranston and Bunker, 2.) Berry and Meg, 3.) Joe and the other boys, 4.) May and the other girls, 5.) Ananiah, 6.) Tess and Gabriella. You could add a narrator, or have each character read the narrative that applies to them. If you are interested in a public production of it, contact Mark R. Turner to see what scripts, offers and permissions are available. Please honor the copyright of this work and purchase the necessary number of books needed for group reading.

From Dust Block by Block, Mark R. Turner, 2011

How You Raise the Edifice

How you raise the edifice
Choosing stones of light
Fitted about that cornerstone
Night builders discarded
For temples made with hands,
Stacked crushing blocks,
Yet tripped over daylight.

But, unquenched,
You piece together the Day
As, one-by-one, day child
Springs from that corner
Sparking and sizzling
Glints of solar prominences,
Exalted into place
As nova beams
Blind out the night.

And rises the household,
Blessing and calling
Into the glory dwell,
Fusion transformed;
Rejoicing this
Is the Day.

Julian, Calif.
September 2007
Psalm 118:22-29
John 1:4-5
I Peter 2:4-10
Hebrews 9:11, 24

A Kid Knocks
in the Night
"Brother Skage, you're
running out of time
and you still have to
deal with Christmas."

A Kid Knocks in the Night

by
Mark R. Turner

Eb Skage is up late. He has struggled and tangled with bows and tape and wrapping paper while trying to compose his Christmas letter until his wits are played out. And how on earth had he allowed the social committee to obligate him for a dozen homemade cookies? "I don't have time for this!" he says out loud. His thoughts are grumbling, "There is too much to get done by Christmas. Well, they're not going to make me go caroling! Of that I am adamant. It's undignified. Me, the head of a corporation, a six ... six-figure salary, mind you ... I'm too nice! That's what it is: too nice and I ought to let a few heads roll. Then they'll ... and all this extra busy work just because my secretary had to have the night off to spend with her brats." He yawns the words out, "Christmas is just too ... Oh ... brother ..." He leans back and lets his eyes close. Snoring ensues and all is calm.

Somewhere in his dreaming a boy is outside the house singing, but not a Christmas carol.

"Are you sleeping? Are you sleeping?
Brother Skage, brother Skage.
Morning bells are ringing.
Morning bells are ringing.
Ding Dong Ding
Ding Dong Ding"

Someone starts bouncing a basketball.

Outside in the glow of Skage's Christmas decorations a kid loiters bouncing his basketball. Even shopping traffic is gone, and his voice echoes off of the cold buildings. He trots up to the big front window of Skage's posh town house and peeks in. "Uh-huh. The old guy finally conked out in that chair."

He dribbles his ball up to Skage's front door and begins knocking. "Knock knock!" he yells. "Yoohoo! Anybody home?"

Skage starts forward in his chair. "Aaag!" He rubs his eyes and yawns. "What's that? Hm... left the lights on." He starts to push himself out of the chair.

"Knock knock!" yells the kid rapping at the door.

Skage wakes fully with a scowl. He hobbles to the front window. "Wh—! Is that a kid on the street? God, I'm walking like an old man." The incessant knocking is rattling him.

"I'm standing at the door knocking," yells the boy. "If anyone hears my voice and opens the door I will come in!"

Skage mimics the voice, "'If anyone hears my voice.' How could anyone help but hear it?" He stops and thinks. "Where have I heard that line before? Ah, so what." He straightens up and stomps to the door. "Must be four in the morning!" Preparing to yell he opens the door.

"Hi! Sure, I'll come in." The kid dribbles his ball into the entry way as if in the heat of a game.

Skage is thrown. "Wha'—What child is this?"

The kid incorporates his song into the game.

"... Morning bells are ringing
Morning bells are ringing
Ding Dong Ding
Ding Dong Ding"

Skage comes to his senses and blows up. "Yeah! You ain't a kiddin', 'morning bells are ringing!' What's the big idea, out playing before the sun comes up? What parent would let his boy come over at this hour? Do you realize I have been up all night with holiday configurations?"

The kid does a trick bounce and keeps the rhythm of the ball going. "Yeah, I saw ya sleeping in that old, stiff chair, Brother Skage?"

Skage pulls back and peers down at him. "Who are you?!"

The kid bounces on and eyes the open door. "Boy, sure is a draft in here, Brother Skage."

"Well, that's because the door is still open, sonny .... Go on. Go on. Out o' here!"

He bounces around Skage. "I am appalled that a gentleman such as your self would turn a little kid out on the street in the middle of the night."

Skage can't keep up with him. "Wh—aat!?" Finally, he gives up, "Oh!" and slams the door shut. "Kids these days ... How do you know my name and what's this 'brother' bit? Just stand still and tell me where you live, and we'll try and get you home safely before I get accused of kidnaping. And quite bouncing that infernal ball!"

The kid spins the ball on his finger and parks it on his hip. "Don't you remember me? I came upon a midnight clear, and you invited me in."

Skage does not appreciate the Christmasy reference. "Oh, yeah? I suppose it was a 'silent night,' too, wasn't it? Did you come to town on a burro?"

"Right!" exulted the kid, but then got serious, "'Course, it's been a long time since we spent any time together."

"Look, sonny, don't you think I'd recognize you if I'd met you before?"

"Not necessarily."

"Wise guy. Well, right now you're supposed to be in your own house asleep."

"But my father sent me to you."

Skage is outraged. "What?! Well, of all the ... Where's my phone? I'm just gonna give this guy a call, right now. What's your number?"

"Just one. I'm all you need."

"Okay, I can search it. What's your father's name, boy?"

The kid speaks very slowly and deliberately so as not to be misunderstood, "Well, ... my mother's name is Mary. And Dad's name is ... Joseph ...

Skage concentrates on his phone search. "Good. Good. What's his last name?"

The kid rolls his eyes and turns around in place. "That was the last name I ever heard."

"Oh, games! Quit playing games with me!" Skage fidgets at his phone. "Okay, what line of work is your dad in?"

The kid looks at him, "Really? He's a carpenter. Don't you remember?"

Skage gets sarcastic, "And, I'll just bet they named you Jesús, didn't they?

"Right!" he congratulates Skage.

Skage straightens up and makes for the door. "Okay, if you're an illegal alien, you'd better scram." He opens it. "Here's the door."

The kid glares at the doorway. "Who else were you expecting on Christmas Eve?"

"The border patrol! Better beat it, kid. Hurry! Andale!"

The kid bounces the ball slowly with emphasis, "Brother Skage, you're running out of time and you still have to deal with Christmas."

"You, sonny, are a nosey brat. I could send you up to juvenile hall for snooping around here."

"Okay, calm down. I know you're having a hard time."

"And don't think you can sweet talk me. You haven't got the slightest idea about the pain and agony of adult decisions. And would you, just cool it with that ball, kid?

He parks the ball again, "Well, at least you could help me."

Skage almost pleads, "That's what I'm trying to do."

"Not just get rid of me," the kid retorts. "Help me celebrate my birthday."

Skage gives up and closes the door. He wearily shuffles to the living room. "Poor kid. This close to Christmas you probably get so many presents you don't know what you got."

The kid follows, looking everything over with interest. "Naa, I usually don't get much."

Skage slumps onto the couch. "What kind of people have you got, anyway? Here, they got two excuses to give you something."

Apparently the kid has been to Sunday School. "Oh, our heavenly Father takes care of us, anyway."

"Hm! Very religious."

"Uh-huh," he says looking around the room. "I like to watch birds."

"What?"

"The birds." He looks at Skage. "Do you like to watch birds, Brother Skage?"

"You can cut the Brother Skage bit and the birds I got no time for. I'm a very busy man and I need my sleep."

But the kid goes on, "Sometimes I imagine funny things. Like, if them ol' birds wore shirts and overalls and sneakers." He laughs.

Skage looks at him. "What the –"

"Then you know what they do? They drive tractors and heap in the beans and tomatoes and potatoes and parsley and rutabagas and pineapples and chow mein and chocolate chips and applesauce and they put it all in a big barn and save it 'til they need it!" He laughs at his joke.

Skage is entertained. "Hey, you're pretty good at that, aren't you?"

"But the birds don't really do that. Because our Father gives them everything they need. And that's how he takes care of us and so you don't need to worry, Brother Skage."

Skage catches himself and gets serious. "Worry? Ha! You don't catch me worrying about anything. Each man for himself. I know my strengths and my weaknesses, and I've got plenty of confidence in what I can do." He looks at the boy taking all this in with such attentiveness. "Now look, boy, you're not so bad. A likable kid. You remind me of ... myself. Now, I'll pass on a bit of learning that'll help you rise above your current situation. See, when you get bigger, you'll find that you don't get anything unless you prove you're worth getting paid a good salary."

"But our Father told me if we follow Him, He'll give us everything we need, even if nobody thinks we're worth anything."

Skage is taken aback. "He told you that, huh? Well, who am I to contradict 'Our Father?' What about getting nothing for Christmas and your birthday on top of it? I'd be raising a ruckus over that."

"Naaaa. It's better to give the presents."

"Well, suppose you don't have anything to give, sonny? With an attitude like that, you aren't going to grow up to be much."

"Oh, I'm gonna be just exactly what I'm supposed to be."

Skage chuckles. "How nice. Let me know if you ever make it."

"Well, see, I came into the world only just for a little while, see. Father says I'm the only one like me and I have something for the world which only I can give. So, I'll be going away after a few years."

This sobers Skage and he observes the boy in a whole new light. "So, ... that's the way it is ... I mean, you have something ..."

"But I won't just leave you," encourages the kid. "I'll give you my ball, so you won't be all alone." He looks at Skage quizzically. "Why do you stay alone?"

"Well, ..." Skage cannot come up with an answer but hatches a plan. "Jesús ... well, how would you like to come and spend some time with me?"

The kid almost laughs, "Duh ... That's what I'm doing. You already invited me when you were a kid. Only you kind of ignored me afterwards." Skage does not get this. The kid picks it up, "Hey! You never wanted to play follow the leader before. Wanna play now?"

"Oh, I don't know, Jesús. Do you think ... well, it might get a little noisy ... playing, I mean. I wouldn't want to wake up the neighbors."

The kid stands askance, "I know why you really don't want to play. You think it's sissy playin' follow the leader."

Skage will not be put in that class. "Nonsense. I'm my own man. I was simply pointing out ..." But there is no way around it. He stands up, "Oh! Alright! Now, I'll be the leader. Understand?"

"No. That wouldn't be right," the kid returns.

"Of course it would be right. This is my house. I know the place better than you and there are places I don't want you to get into and you'd start making a ruckus and so there."

"Oh, I know all through your house," announces the kid. "I thought you and me were friends."

Skage appeals to him in his best negotiation skill, "We can be friends ... fella ... but ..." He throws up his hands. "Oh, go on, for the love of Pete, be the leader. But don't cause a ruckus!"

"Great!" The kid does a trick with the ball and offers it to Skage. "Here. You hold the ball." He lunges it into Skage's middle and trots away. "Now do what I do!"

Skage takes off after him. "Well not so fast. Wait up."

"Do a somersault here!"

Skage stops. "Wait. Are you crazy?"

"You promised!"

"Oh!" exclaims Skage as he carefully gets down. "If I promised—" With groans he rolls through a somersault for the first time in over thirty years.

The kid starts hopping with glee. "Hop around like this!"

"Look, I did your somersault—"

"Hop!" the kid commands. "Loosen up, buddy!"

Skage begins hopping. "Oh, sure!" He begins to snicker. "You're the big leader! Ha!"

"You know how to pirouette?" says the kid performing one.

"Peer a what?"

"Like this!" He performs another one. "Come on!"

Skage actually tries one. "Woo ha ha ... I'm getting dizzy ...!"

"Bounce the ball!"

Skage laughs at his clumsiness. "I'm bouncing, I"m bouncing!"

The kid opens the door and hops out onto the porch. "Out the door!"

Skage skids to a halt. "Whoah! Not out on the porch!"

"Come on, Brother Skage."

"You know what I said! Get back in here!"

"You said I was the leader," the kid appeals to him. "You gotta follow the leader!"

Skage cringes and glances at the neighbors' houses. "Would you keep your voicc down!" he whispers.

"I know my way around here," the kid reassures him. "You don't have to be afraid of the neighbors."

"Shush! I said. Get back in here!" Skage is getting desperate.

"Just follow me," says the kid, then adds another incentive. "We can go fishing!"

This gives Skage pause. "Fishing! Are you nuts?" He sputters, "Fine. I'll get you some fish and some nuts if you get back here right now!"

"So, if you won't play follow the leader," proposes the kid, "you gotta play hide and seek! You're it!" He starts to run farther out.

Skage is aghast. "If ... if you get back inside, I'll see what I can do to give you a break in this world."

The kid is farther out now and his yell echoes, "I won't be hard to find. Come and get me!"

Skage still hopes to lure him back, "Jesús! I have a few connections who could make it right for you."

But the kid is out of sight now. "If you seek me, you'll find me!"

Skage calls into the neighborhood, "Jesús! I'll not be made a fool of!" He waits for a response. "It's getting cold, now." He listens and scans the shadows down the block. "Jesús, my offer still stands. ... Door is still open. ... Jesús!"

About a Live Reading of this Scene

"A Kid Knocks in the Night" was originally produced as the final scene in Mark's stage play "The Spirit Fooled Christmas" in the early 1970's. The full play has been produced numerous times over the years and may eventually be offered in its entirety as a book. Mark and his wife Donna perform this scene as audio theater on Mark's YouTube channel at https://horizongate.org/KidKnocks .

Two people can have fun reading this scene aloud as a short offering for a seasonal gathering. If you are interested in a public production of it or the full play, contact Mark R. Turner to see what scripts, offers and permissions are available. Please honor the copyright of this work and purchase the necessary number of books needed for a live reading.

Commentary on "A Kid Knocks in the Night"

[Note: This piece first appeared in the Horizongate.org blog as an introduction to the audio theater rendition of the scene found on YouTube at https://horizongate.org/KidKnocks .]

Regardless of the many positive and negative views of Christmas the central metaphor and the many symbols of the faith narrative is a wake-up call to humanity.

In every era humanity has tried to settle things into the equilibrium of what we have thought was the final ideal state of being. Today Western culture looks more complex, but we still live to achieve goals of comfort, control, and self-possession. We are frustrated by the competition, variables, and interferences of everyone else striving in their own ways to achieve the same ideal. The freedom we might have gotten a glimpse of as children quickly dissipates and we put it behind us in our pursuit of the vision that is so elusive.

In the audio theater piece above the Kid coming in the night is that True Self which we wish we could be. When he knocks on our door and disturbs our privacy we resist, though we still have a yearning for that "something" calling us outside of our safe boundaries. This is the story of the Christ Child, inconvenient and disruptive, but representing the vast unknown possibilities beyond our finite constructs.

The faith narrative of Christmas is about that coming, knocking in the night, and calling us out to a destiny which is so much more than our current state of being that it is the Mystery of Goodness. When we wake up and risk stepping out into that Mystery we become the signs, the symbols that Goodness is really incarnating humanity.

Where Can Seeing Be?

I lay me down all dark and cold
Between the winter's pallid fold
And groaned the weary prayer of old,
"Where can seeing be?"

Will night time ever come to end?
Can I the bondage never bend?
The suffocating dark amend?
"Where can seeing be?"

Speak over wasteland strewn with bone
Where pilgrims fell on journeys lone
To grasp and make the day their own.
"Where can seeing be?"

The specks of light afar will tell
The story I have craved so well
Of sunrise reaching into hell
"Where can seeing be?"

So, coming I have groped for Thee.
A star arising beckoned me
To journey from another sea
"Where can seeing be?"

And standing weary at your door
The mud you wash from my eyes sore
And wake me from the sightless war.
I Thy face can see.

El Cajon, Calif.
December 1999

Where Can Seeing Be?

an Advent carol

Mark R. Turner — Mark R. Turner

Power of the Tiny Particle

[Note: This essay first appeared on the blog of horizongate.org in December 2020]

Sometimes, when saturated with national and global news, we tend to focus on that larger picture and neglect our main responsibility on the microlevel of our personal relationships and local community. Voting and demonstrating about the larger issues are good and important community responsibilities, but most of our effectiveness is in the place where we live. We can be confident that our quality of contribution there will influence the larger picture especially as it harmonizes with contributions of others exponentially over time.

But few seem to discover, accept, or appreciate their status as a minute particle important to God's reality, the reality that is far beyond the national level. On God's level social and political hierarchy is non-existent.

About Christmas

Christmas is a celebration of an obscure, seemingly insignificant peasant couple giving birth to a fragile baby in an animal enclosure of a minor country owned by a global empire. Only many centuries later would a major part of the world celebrate it as a holy day. Mary, Joseph and the baby Jesus may not have been fully aware of their place at the culmination of centuries and the beginning of profound changes. But they moved ahead in what they were given to live.

Most do not like the fact that progress is minute, incremental, and slow. But we can see that the cumulative constancy of small particles over time moves the greater Body along. It is viral and exponential. However, those who do sense the value of being a minute particle of the whole usually operate in the love ethic.

The Love Ethic

Not just an emotional response, the love ethic is an orientation to life. I occasionally recognize it in myself when I labor long and hard on works of art and writing even though I know they may be viewed and read only by a few. Hoping to contribute to the common good, I experience joy when someone receives what I offer, and grief when the contribution is rejected or ignored. But I can always return to a kind of wonder that if I make or write something presenting truths I have discovered, someone somewhere, now or in the future, will be helped in their own awakening. This love ethic is the energy and life that makes me a functioning part of the larger Body.

Talk to any effective leader in the public arena, or even the small group, and they will tell you about the patient, marathon attitude required to negotiate progress increment by increment. They will speak of something like faith in the face of repeated failure. You can think of your own examples, but some of my current examples are John Lewis, Joe Biden, Stacey Abrams, people who serve more than they receive, who "go beyond the call of duty", who postpone their own comfort and benefits. This includes anyone who lays down their life for others, a love Jesus said was the greatest.

Where to Find This Kind

Most of those who live by the love ethic are unknown except by a few — hence the designation as "minute particles in the whole."

The parent who daily fixes dinner for the family.

The person who keeps recyclables separated.

The driver who allows the other car into their lane.

The person who spontaneously gives a dollar to a beggar on the street.

Those who wear the mask even though it is uncomfortable, and some say its effect on the pandemic is minimal.

Being a sympathetic listener.

Giving words of comfort to someone who cannot benefit you.

Choosing optimism to orient your efforts countering trouble even when others think you are unrealistic.

The person who calms another's fears.

The small business which maintains generosity despite small profits because of its mission to help people.

The artist who strives for the highest quality even when the mediocre "will do," or chooses a project more for the important message than the commercial potential.

The person who takes the time, effort, and risk to demonstrate in the streets for a good cause.

The writer who creates a poem, novel, play, screenplay, or blog post not because they expect to get rich and famous, but because some truth inspires them to tell whoever will pause to consider it and be helped in their journey ahead.

You probably recognize things about yourself in this little bit of an infinite list.

Persevering in the Good

The love ethic is why some people keep productive and active even when they could afford to just play and indulge themselves, or who just deserve to retire. It is what made Jesus walk from village to village telling stories, healing, and teaching even when he was fatigued and threatened with arrest, torture, and assassination.

Contributing to the unstoppable ground swell of goodness and life is usually done in minute deeds. It is like the mustard seed which Jesus pointed out, though seemingly insignificant, is irrepressible. Once it has started in the garden it cannot be easily eradicated, becomes a refuge to the birds of the air and drops its seed to raise up more goodness (Matthew 13:31).

We are the seeds continuing the exponential growth of the new creation which Isaiah prophesied would cover the earth "as the waters cover the sea" (Isaiah 11:9).

Sprout to Stars, Mark R. Turner, 2015

At this Time

At this time
The clamor rests awhile
And breathing slows to give up
Just a pause and make
The pressures wait a night,
Perceive a music in the stars.

Someone in the crowds
Found a corner
Where she had labor,
Her worried husband helped
The child exit, enter
Into good soil.

We, oblivious,
Taken up with pressing things,
Pursuing world affairs,
Let seeds sprout as they may,
One no more important
Than the next.

That One unknown
Rose slowly through the soil
Midst trampling,
Drought,
Consuming browsers
And blossomed.

So that, far away now,
Nothing quenches
Spreading, verdant foliage
Planted long ago

Upon a corner no one watched
Except some laborers
Pausing for the music
In the sky.

Julian, Calif.
October 2006

Unconditional Love

[Note: This essay first appeared on the blog of horizongate.org in December 2023]

This is the season when masses of people make special effort to express Love. I encourage everyone to participate in this. I know that much of our efforts overemphasize materialism in "opening the presents", and consuming extra food and drink. But it is possible for us to refine that, taking the opportunity to demonstrate and experience the real, core Love.

In the other extreme, some take advantage of "the season" for the opportunity to preach an exclusionary message that Jesus is born only to be the sacrifice for all the sins of whoever does what the preacher specifies. Either you must be punished for your state of sin in the lake of fire, or you can qualify for Jesus to placate God.

Richard Rohr said in a talk "... we make God the Father the great big 'ogre in the sky' who can't love his children naturally, organically, inherently, but has to be talked into it ... [We] made the great mystery of the transformational power of love into a heavenly transaction between Jesus and God the Father, in which God the Father comes out not looking very good."

This is not the Love that Jesus revealed, and to which humanity is trying to awaken at Christmas time. I invite you to allow Love to massage that Christmas wish into your real, daily world. Jesus reveals the unconditional Love that liberates everyone to realize our membership in something far greater than ourselves or religion, and to participate in growing, expanding Goodness. Love being unconditional makes it absolutely powerful, liberating and miraculously mysterious. It is not intellectual, although it inspires us mentally and physically. We know it spiritually. Allowing ourselves to awaken to this causes positive transformation.

Transformational Power of Love

This is only talk and verbal intellect until it is meditated upon and becomes a hunger.

Quiet the cacophony of the world around you and wait for the meaning of the words "unconditional Love" to open you to possibility.

Your inner, True Self begins to sense a difference and you begin to go about your daily life wondering how this newness will alter your experience of living.

You return to your personal contemplative times and renew the sense of it, while beginning to make decisions with the new point of view.

Perhaps you are unaware of changing, but Love is transforming you, growing you into someone broader, expanding, ascending.

You grow more aware of communing with this energy which you unite with as the True Person, the One incarnated with the Spirit which creates the universe. Is it your True Self, Jesus, God, or all? Differentiation becomes less and less important.

You gradually see yourself as a member of a Whole and learn to appreciate your influence in even the smallest details. You become more compassionate toward errors and corrections, always moving on, recognizing that this transformation is part of the progression of all things, not only your initiative.

May your Christmas and Hanukkah presents, meals and parties celebrate unconditional Love expanding us as God's universal Body.

Our Mirror in the Manger, Mark R. Turner, 2017

Going Into Bethlehem

Going into Bethlehem
To see this thing
Of which we were told,
We gazed on the baby,
Another of us born anew.

The world did not know him, or us,
For it did not appear
What he would be,
Or how we would become him.

We beheld ourselves gazing
As into a mirror, yet darkly,
For we knew not what new creation
Lay through this door.

Day following day
Would inevitably grow
From this manger to appear
When we would see him as he is,
The precedent by God's grace
Elevating us through himself,
Making us the body
God incarnates.

So, we look from this plain far beyond,
Lifting off the previous world,
Sojourning through his open portal,
Seeing ourselves as him ahead,
Hearing the call to come forth
As a seed leaves earth
Into sky of light and wind,

Being new
More than we can
Think or imagine.

San Diego, Calif.
December 2014 - May, 2015

The Wrappings of Christmas

[Note: This essay first appeared on the blog of horizongate.org in November 2022]

The Christmas collection of cultural traditions is enjoyed by people around the world even as cultures vary and change. To create and operate within cultures is a human invariant.

Human invariants include eating, sleeping, working to make home, communicating in a native language, relating in a society, Love. We create cultural ways to accommodate the invariants. One invariant is all people's awareness or wonder about something beyond our materiality and we create religions to facilitate this contemplation.

Religions are cultural ways in which we express spiritual awareness, and most people equate their cultural way with spiritual ultimates. This does not mean the ultimates are only cultural, but we tend to substitute our cultural wrapping for that which is the True beyond the wrapping, often sanctifying cultural aspects along with the ultimates.

For instance, some Christmas symbolism combines details from the Gospels to hold a sacred picture of the well-clothed holy family in a cozy enclosure with peaceful animals surrounded by rugged people of the earth on one side and opulent, exotic royalty on the other. Some resist any suggestion that this is probably not how it looked.

Church Culture

I grew up in an American subculture of Pentecostal Church that held many cultural things as sacred Truth which actually were not ultimates: no smoking, no dancing, no alcoholic drinking, no card gambling, no swearing, only heterosexual marriage, proselytizing as a command from God, the printed Bible as inerrant, "the End Times" including a certain order of cosmic events culminating with a lake of fire (hell) for all who do not accept Jesus as the only Son of God and heaven with gold-paved streets for all who qualify.

Today there are people building a power base to force their religious culture on entire nations, i.e.: Christian Nationalism, the Taliban. Unfortunately, too many Christians hold philosophical justification for behaviors contrary to Christ as a means to enforce their culture on the world, such as dictatorial rulers, subjugation of selected kinds of people, terrorism, physical and verbal abuse, and murder (aka "execution"). This parallels the circumstances surrounding the Nativity story we celebrate this season.

We Want the Ultimate Paradise

Perhaps some see the glow of an ultimate paradise beyond current circumstances and take it upon themselves to make it happen now. They do not want to wait for God to nurture us toward that glow; they want it in their "lifetime".

The alternative is to actually live Goodness in the here and now. Without seeing the material fulfillment in our lifetime, we can make our contribution as a small part in the long lineage toward it. We acknowledge our kinship with past and future people who all reach for this destiny.

Distinguishing between ultimates and cultural symbols of those ultimates helps our progress toward peace and unity for all humanity. Acknowledging that all people have capacity for the truly sacred helps relax our grip on symbols, rituals, and exclusive behaviors. Acknowledging that God is present "over there" as well as "with us" does not in any way diminish the Truth that our culture represents. Recognizing ultimates represented by other cultures can enrich awareness of the truths we hold dear in ours. This can relieve us of a colonial "mission" to dominate other cultures or proselytize people out of their culture into ours. Instead, we will promote each other's growth into the ultimates we all seek.

Jesus demonstrated this attitude in his conversation with the Samaritan woman at the well (John 4) where he said the ways and places we worship do not matter because God is Spirit and desires us to worship in Spirit and Truth.

God Is More Than My Gifts

While the church of my early years was very cultural, still embedded in it was the realization that God is more than all these symbols and add-on cultural imperatives. The faithfulness of many within the cultural religion to teach that God is more than culture provided the freedom to grow and discover the expansiveness of the ultimates which all humanity senses are invariants.

The teaching that God is more helps us to realize and commune with the True Ultimate. As humans it is our nature to use symbols drawn from the world we know to enjoy communion with God. But I recognize that ***God, to be God, cannot be contained by my cultural symbols, rituals, explanations, or structures.*** To enjoy the freedom of the infinite God, I am holding lightly to my helpful symbols which loft me into the greater expanse of eternity where I will eventually let go of my tether to all the helps I have been given.

Culture, then, is a gift that we can hold respectfully without fear of appreciating the gifts of others. As **Howard Thurman** demonstrated in his **intercultural church** and **Gandhi** in his **interfaith community**, we can even benefit from experiencing one another's gifts.

The Birthing Story

The primordial invariant is our awakening to creation's emanation from God. We vary in all the behaviors and symbols we use to pursue that awakening. My personal experience is an affirmation within my deepest perception that this awakening is growth toward Goodness, and that it is initiated and secured by the Will beyond my constructs or descriptions. It is not a matter only of my mortal self, but of the Will that is bringing forth materiality. The symbolism of birthing is an important indicator of the process we are in, as in Jesus' metaphor of being born (John 3), and Paul's words about all of creation groaning in labor birthing what must come, the revelation of the children of God (Romans 8:19-23). As in "the Lord's Prayer", praying for that Will to be done is acknowledging our reality as members of and harmonizing with Creation emerging from God.

The story of Jesus' nativity illustrates some of the ways we block the birth and growth of humanity:

- cultural oppression of women (Mary could have been legally executed for her pregnancy outside of marriage.)
- The life-threatening requirement to travel to Bethlehem and be "registered" by the empire
- Herod's genocidal attempts to kill a potential rival by killing all children of two years and younger in and around Bethlehem
- Jesus' family fleeing to Egypt as refugees
- Jesus growing up in the oppression of an occupied country

But the supremacy of Life coming forth is the outcome of the story. Losses and defeats notwithstanding, the sprout emerges, grows and multiplies; the unnoticed mustard seed grows into the largest tree; the unseen yeast permeates the loaf. Jesus' behavior and teaching, wrapped in his culture, demonstrate the primordial invariant resulting in the thriving of Life.

Another Shoreline, Mark R. Turner, 1990-2019

The Wise Men

The wise men, the kings, Magi,
Distant descendants of old Adam
Far to the east in lands unthought of;
Audacious entrepreneurs,
Risk takers like children,
The few strange wealthy
With libraries and time
Enough to dredge the records of those long dead;
Moved by shards of truth still strewn in the memory of their race
Mount a privately funded expedition
Across frontiers
Through suspicious tribes
Strange tongues needing subtle diplomacy;
Independent ambassadors
Unsent by an unknowing people;
A caravan bearing sustenance for man and beast,
And charts of knowledge preserved in signs of the sky,
The priceless scrolls of Hebrew origin;
Packing gifts for tolls
But treasures for tribute
To one who rises,
Who pops the old man's chrysalis
And takes dominion of all peoples,
Time, land and sea and stars.

Spring Valley, Calif.
December 1998

Don't miss out!

Visit the website below and you can sign up to receive emails whenever Mark R. Turner publishes a new book. There's no charge and no obligation.

https://books2read.com/r/B-A-AIMYC-WPJKF

Also by Mark R. Turner

The Future Seed
Give Us this Day
Beautify, Oh : fifty-one poems
You After All
From Here to Kingdom Come
The Lost Kids Spy Christmas
Pulling Back the Earth
Your Table of Creation
Marking the Journey: Holding the Past, Reaching Ahead
Verse and Visions from Advent, Christmas and Epiphany
Ray of Lightning
Revival
Monthly Stimulants Volume 1
Tales to Cultivate the Soul: 11 Alternative Stories
Treats & Retreats for Christmas

Watch for more at linktr.ee/markarturner.

About the Author

Mark Turner is a visual artist, filmmaker, writer and artistic leader. He has produced and taught in five major regions of the globe as the director of Horizon Gate Productions, a non-profit arts organization which he co-founded with his wife in 1981. His emphasis has been in multi-media to tell stories and produce contemplative experiences using his visuals, poetry and soundtracks. He is currently creating tangible and digital art of inspirational and metaphorical images which he then re-purposes as motion graphics films with rich sound tracks of his poetry, sound effects and music. All this can be exhibited together in a conversational atmosphere called the Film Gallery Cafe.

Read more at linktr.ee/markarturner.

www.ingramcontent.com/pod-product-compliance
Lightning Source LLC
LaVergne TN
LVHW090125160826
845673LV00015B/1013
9798230673453